She'll Be Comin' 'Round the Mountain

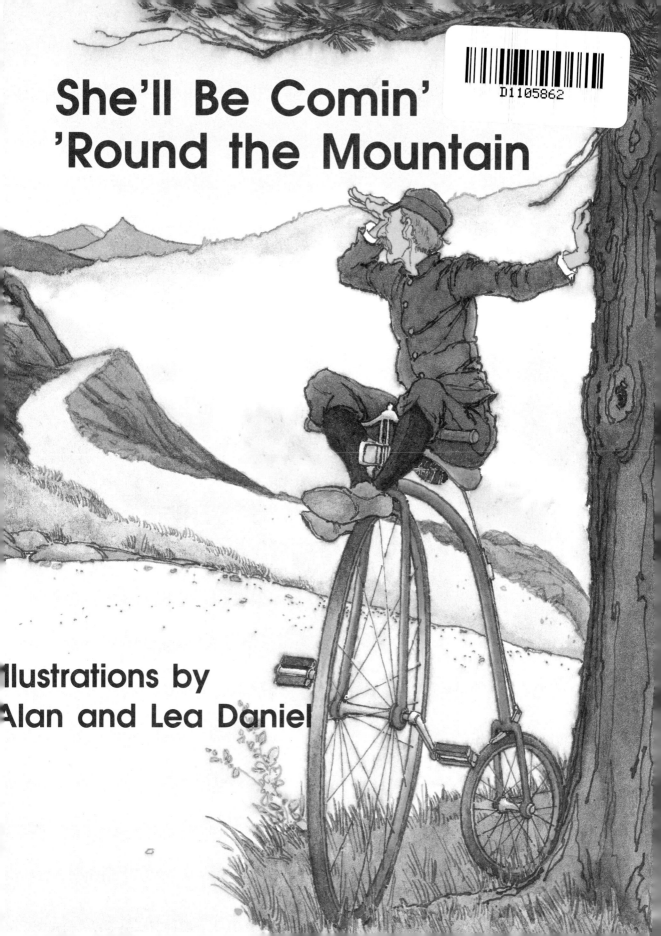

Illustrations by
Alan and Lea Daniel

She'll be comin' 'round the mountain
     when she comes. (Toot! Toot!)
She'll be comin' 'round the mountain
     when she comes. (Toot! Toot!)
She'll be comin' 'round the mountain,
she'll be comin' 'round the mountain,
she'll be comin' 'round the mountain
     when she comes. (Toot! Toot!)

She'll be drivin' six white horses
    when she comes. (Whoa back!)
She'll be drivin' six white horses
    when she comes. (Whoa back!)
She'll be drivin' six white horses,
she'll be drivin' six white horses,
she'll be drivin' six white horses
    when she comes. (Whoa back!)

Oh, we'll all go out to greet her
when she comes. (Hi, there!)
Oh, we'll all go out to greet her
when she comes. (Hi, there!)
Oh, we'll all go out to greet her,
oh, we'll all go out to greet her,
oh, we'll all go out to greet her
when she comes. (Hi, there!)

Then we'll kill the old red rooster
  when she comes. (Squawk, squawk!)
Then we'll kill the old red rooster
  when she comes. (Squawk, squawk!)
Then we'll kill the old red rooster,
then we'll kill the old red rooster,
then we'll kill the old red rooster
  when she comes. (Squawk, squawk!)

And we'll all have chicken and dumplings
   when she comes. (Yum, yum!)
And we'll all have chicken and dumplings
   when she comes. (Yum, yum!)
And we'll all have chicken and dumplings,
and we'll all have chicken and dumplings,
and we'll all have chicken and dumplings
   when she comes. (Yum, yum!)

Oh, she'll wear her red pajamas
  when she comes. (Scratch, scratch!)
Oh, she'll wear her red pajamas
  when she comes. (Scratch, scratch!)
Oh, she'll wear her red pajamas,
oh, she'll wear her red pajamas,
oh, she'll wear her red pajamas
  when she comes. (Scratch, scratch!)

Oh, she'll have to sleep with Grandma
when she comes. (Snore, snore!)
Oh, she'll have to sleep with Grandma
when she comes. (Snore, snore!)
Oh, she'll have to sleep with Grandma,
oh, she'll have to sleep with Grandma,
oh, she'll have to sleep with Grandma
when she comes. (Snore, snore!)

She'll be drivin' six white horses
when they go. (Bye, there!)
She'll be drivin' six white horses
when they go. (Bye, there!)
She'll be drivin' six white horses,
she'll be drivin' six white horses,
she'll be drivin' six white horses
when they go. (Bye, there!)